Somebunny Love

By Lisa Soland

With Illustrations
by Leanna Hewitt Sain

Climbing Angel Publishing

Knoxville, Tennessee

Climbing Angel Publishing
P.O. Box 32381
Knoxville, Tennessee 37930
http://www.ClimbingAngel.com

Manufactured in the United States of America
Book design by Zachary Hodges
Edited by Darnell Arnoult and Sue Dunlap
Cover photo by Lisa Soland, Cover models Charlotte Dobens and Chesterly
Special thanks to the Oak Ridge Animal Shelter
Internal Angel Logo by Adelyn Sterbenz, 6 years old, from Spring Grove, Illinois.

ISBN: 978-0-9965721-2-5
Library of Congress Control Number: 2016943763

In memory of Geisha, Thumper, Simon Peter, Pooka,
Elmer Fudd, Bugs Bunny, Nutter Butter, Oreo, Wildfire and
all their descendants...

Foreword

by Pastor Sam Polson

Awkward...that is how I felt...but it didn't last long.

Yes, I am ashamed to say I felt a little awkward when my good friend, Lisa Soland, excitedly asked me one afternoon during a visit in the church office if she could read to me her final draft for this book, *Somebunny to Love.* I mean really, was a dignified and theologically trained pastor like myself supposed to sit quietly in his ministerial inner sanctum and listen to a story about a bunny?

Yes, that is exactly what I was supposed to do, and am I ever glad I was privileged to do it! Within a few minutes I was completely captivated by this beautiful story. Perhaps as a pastor I should refer to it as a parable, because in fact that is what it is...a simple, understandable, earthly story that communicates the timeless spiritual truth of unconditional love. Lisa has given a gift to every person, regardless of his or her age, who is blessed to read this book.

This story draws you into the bittersweet season of a child's life, while at the same time draws from you a deep gratitude for the privilege of participating in the most divine activity on this planet...loving others expecting nothing in return. When we make the choice to give that gift, we find we have given to ourselves the greatest gift of all!

Sam Polson, Lead Pastor

West Park Baptist Church
Knoxville, Tennessee

Somebunny to Love

Somebunny to Love

Some people like the *feeling* part of love best. They like it so much that it becomes all they want. But the feeling part comes and goes. And when it goes, some people think they've lost their love. But if they've lost it, it wasn't real. It was just the *feeling* part. Real love never goes away.

Real love is not like you see on TV. You can flip through the channels as many times as you'd like all day, every day, but you won't find real love there. What happens to you when you watch TV is only the feeling you get from watching other people pretend they're experiencing real love.

Real love happens in your *own life*. It begins when you're bold enough to say to some other person or living thing, "I'm going to take care of you no matter what." Then real love happens when you follow through on that promise.

1

Real love is like the time my father brought home a rabbit from the shelter. We named her Geisha because she had black around her eyes and looked like a Geisha girl from Japan. But she didn't act like a Geisha girl from Japan. Our Geisha was not shy. She bit, and when Geisha bit, she bit hard. And it hurt.

We had our own ideas of how our new rabbit should behave. We wanted a playmate for our other rabbit, Thumper, who was easy to love. Thumper liked us and behaved as a good bunny should. When we petted him, he licked our hands because he couldn't receive love without giving some back.

All Geisha did was chase Thumper and when she caught him, she bit him with her razor sharp teeth. Thumper was shocked at her behavior. He wasn't used to being bitten.

We tried to be patient. We thought she would change. We thought one day she would be the kind of rabbit we could be proud of. Then one day Geisha bit me for the last time, and my mother wasn't patient anymore. She was angry.

"Charlotte, get Geisha's box and put some straw in it while I call your father." She dialed the phone as I left the room.

I thought about how hopeful we were when my dad first brought Geisha home.

But she didn't turn out like we thought. What could we do? I felt very sad. I felt as if we'd failed somehow.

I carried the box into the kitchen and looked up at my mother who was still on the phone. She wasn't talking anymore. She was listening. When she listened, I knew my father was saying something important.

"Alright," she said. "That's what we'll do then. Love you too." She hung up the phone. "Charlotte, your daddy says if we bring Geisha back to the shelter they will put her to sleep."

"For good?" I asked.

"Yes. They can't give people pets that bite."

"Because it hurts." I rubbed my wrist where we could still see the teeth marks.

"Your daddy says we need to change the way we've been thinking about Geisha. We've been thinking about what *she* can do for *us*. Now we're going to think about what *we* can do for *her*."

"I don't understand."

"You will not be feeding her anymore. I will, and I'll put on the gloves to do it. Your father and I will make sure she has everything she needs. We'll give her water and let her out of the cage for exercise. And hope for the best."

"So this is like feeding the homeless people downtown and not expecting them to ever feed us back."

"That's exactly right. Real love is being okay with not getting anything in return."

"I see. What can I do, Mom?"

"You can love her, Charlotte. Just love her. And pray."

So that became our new plan, and we

stuck to it. It's a good thing we did because it wasn't long after that when Geisha stopped biting us. And she stopped biting Thumper too, which made him a very happy bunny. When they played together, Thumper could relax and not worry about being attacked.

Soon, I was feeding the bunnies all by myself again. I gave them hay for their digestion, pellets, and sometimes kale, which was their favorite. Once in a great while, I cut them an inch-long piece of banana, which they devoured instantly, like candy.

You can learn a lot about something or someone by watching and listening. One thing I noticed about Thumper and Geisha was that when they were extremely happy, they would jump straight up in the air and twist. This is called a binky, and it is a simple expression of great joy.

I loved when my rabbits did this. It made me laugh and when I laughed, they would stop and listen to me laughing. They seemed to love my laugh as much as I loved their binkies. We would go back and forth like that for quite some time, binky then laugh, over and over, until we couldn't stand it anymore.

One night when we were all asleep, I woke to the sound of a loud banging. I couldn't figure out where it was coming from. I looked out the window thinking it might have been the

neighbor slamming a car door, over and over again. But everything out front seemed still and quiet.

I walked downstairs and noticed that the sound was coming from the deck behind the house where the bunnies lived. I opened the back door and saw Thumper slamming his two back feet against the floor of his cage. Something must have frightened him, like a raccoon or a skunk or something. I later read that "thumping" is a way rabbits signal each other when there's danger.

We also learned that rabbits live longer when they are kept *inside* the house. So, because we loved them and wanted them to live as long as possible, we moved their two cages indoors. And the thumping in the middle of the night stopped.

Thumper and Geisha absolutely loved to be petted on the head. Geisha would hunker down against the floor and let us pet her for hours on end. Sometimes my arm felt like it might fall off my body from exhaustion before Geisha grew tired of having her head petted. She was a taker. She took love.

Thumper, however, took and gave love. You couldn't pet him without him licking you back. It was as if he would rather die than take our family's love without offering some kindness to us in return. But not Geisha. She was absolutely fine taking. And she was good at it.

Most people don't realize how truly great rabbits are. They have unique personalities, each and every one of them. They can easily live as long as a pet dog. Think about that before you go out and get yourself one because once you do, once you tell a rabbit, "I'm going to take care of you no matter what," you have to stick to it, even though toward the end, taking care of them gets hard.

That's how it was with my bunnies. They had been doing so well for so long that I was beginning to think that they were always going to be with us. Then Geisha, the younger rabbit, got sick. She wasn't eating much, and that wasn't good.

My mom and I took her to the veterinarian, and the vet said she had a bad bacteria in her body. They gave Geisha a shot and sent us home with some medicine. We were faithful in doing what the vet told us to do, but Geisha wasn't getting better.

Then one night Thumper became disoriented. He turned 'round and 'round in his cage, like he didn't know which way was up or down or right or left. The next morning he was falling over on his side. We took him to the vet, and the vet agreed that Thumper needed to be put to sleep. For good.

I did not want to leave Thumper's side. My mother let me go by myself into the back room of the animal hospital. The vet gently placed a gas mask over Thumper's little face. It all happened so slowly. Slowly and gracefully, with honor, Thumper went to sleep with my arms wrapped lovingly around him.

My tears dropped on the cold, sterile metal table on which my bunny now rested. The vet handed me tissue after tissue until there were no tissues left. And then my bunny, who could not receive my love without giving me some back, was dead. I couldn't believe it.

My mom and I brought him home and placed him in a shoebox. When Dad returned from work, he dug a hole in our yard and we put Thumper into the ground and covered him up with dirt. I cried the entire time. But when it was over I was surprised that I got through it, and I knew that I was going to be okay. After all, Thumper was an old bunny. He had lived a full life.

The next day Geisha took a turn for the worse. She could hardly hold her head up, so she laid it across her food dish. It was so sad. I didn't know what to do or how to feel.

I sat beside her cage and told her that I loved her, over and over again. I prayed, "Dear God, please don't let Geisha die. Thumper died and that should be enough. Please heal Geisha so she can go on living a good life with me."

My mother came into the room and said, "Charlotte, get the box and fill it with straw."

"Okay," I said.

We got into the car and made the journey back to the vet. They called us into the examining room, and I lifted a limp Geisha out of the box. I tried to hold her up as best as I could. I was sure the cold, metal table was uncomfortable, so I stood as close as I could to reassure her, and Geisha rested her heavy head on my wrist.

It broke my heart. I told her that she was a good bunny and that I loved her so very much.

The doctor came in and gave her another shot and sent us home again with some more medicine.

That night, I did not leave her side.

"It doesn't seem fair," I told my mother. "We buried one bunny last night, and now, only one day later, this bunny is not doing well either."

"Pray, Charlotte. Ask God for what you need."

I prayed and I prayed. "Please God, let Geisha live." That's what I needed, I thought. I needed pets that don't die so I didn't have to keep going through this sadness and grief.

I tried to feed her but she wouldn't eat. Not even an inch worth of banana interested her. That's when I knew we were in trouble. She climbed into my lap and rested her very heavy head on my leg. My heart was breaking but there was nothing I could do.

"You miss Thumper, don't you, girl?" I asked. "You miss your friend." She looked up at me then licked my hand. I couldn't believe it. Then she licked my wrist as if to say she was sorry for all those bites, that she really did love me but just didn't know how to show it. I told her I kept no record of those bites because I had forgiven her long ago. Then I told her that I loved her and that I always would.

Suddenly, Geisha darted out of my lap onto the hardwood floor, but the floor was slippery so she didn't go very far. I quickly picked her up and placed her on the carpet because she seemed to want to go somewhere, fast. She took one step and then fell over on her side and died.

I was stunned. I had no idea what had just happened. I had no idea why she had to die only one day after Thumper. I had no idea how I was going to live without my two, most precious friends. They were gone. My brain seemed to shut off and my body felt numb.

My mother put Geisha into a shoebox, and my father dug another hole next to Thumper's grave. We placed her into the ground. I picked up some dirt and threw it hard into the hole, on top of the box.

I looked at my mother and father and asked them loudly, "Why do we bother loving something? Why? It seems like a big waste of time to me!"

Then I ran to my room and slammed the door behind me. I wanted to be alone so no one would talk me out of being sad. I think my parents knew this, so they didn't come after me and try to talk. I fell asleep crying.

The next morning I woke up and went downstairs to feed my bunnies, but they weren't there.

That night I went to feed them again, and they were still not there.

Again and again I forgot that life had changed without my permission, and there was no going back. I missed them, but I was afraid to talk about how much I missed them because it all felt so silly. They were just rabbits, after all. What would happen if one of my parents died? If I hurt this much because of a bunny or two, what would I feel when I lost my mom or dad?

I was running into things, like the wall. I was stubbing my toes, bumping into doorknobs, forgetting books at school. Homework was not getting done. It was as if everything in the world had taken a giant step forward, and now it was all in my way because I hadn't taken a giant step forward with it.

That's how death is. When it happens it makes itself known, and for a time it gets in the way of the living.

The worst part about Thumper and Geisha's deaths was how they taught me to stop loving. "If you don't want to get hurt, don't love things so much," death whispered in my ear. So I didn't.

I stopped being nice to people. I started envying my friends at school whose pets were still alive. I stopped listening to my mother when she asked me to help her with the dishes. I shouted out loud to no one in particular, "What good is it all? Why bother?"

But I noticed something rather interesting. While I wasn't being very kind to others around me, my mother and father were still being kind to me. Even though I didn't want to eat, they encouraged me by placing food in front of me anyway, like I had done for Geisha. Even though I didn't want to talk to God, they prayed for me, like I had prayed for the bunnies.

Sometimes things die, even when you pray for them not to, because God has a bigger plan that only He can see. It makes our lives better to trust in Him and His plan.

*L*ife went on even though I didn't want it to. Eventually things did return to normal, or as close to normal as life could be without good friends at my side. But I had made up my mind. I was no longer going to love. It seemed pointless.

Then one night, while I was drying the dishes, my father appeared in the kitchen carrying a puppy – an adorable, playful, big-pawed puppy with black around his eyes just like Geisha. Without hesitation, I ran to this little dog and gave him kisses upon more kisses. I hugged my father and my mother, and thanked them for every single thing – for thinking for me when I couldn't think for myself. And most of all, for loving me when I didn't deserve it.

When I got into bed that night, I asked God to help me always love that dog, especially when it got hard to love him, when I didn't *feel* like it anymore.

I said, "God, if this dog gets sick and I have to nurse him, to love him, to lose him, I will need your help. I will need Your help, always, in learning how to be in this world with a heart that breaks inside of my chest on a regular basis because it is busy loving as You would have us love."

And though I never actually heard God answer my prayer out loud, I have always kept a Bible on my nightstand. When I need to be reminded of His definition of love, I look it up in 1st Corinthians, Chapter 13.

"Love is patient, love is kind. It does not envy, it does not boast, it is not proud. It does not dishonor others, it is not self-seeking, it is not easily angered, it keeps no record of wrongs... It always protects, always trusts, always hopes, always perseveres. Love never fails."

Never. And when God says never, He means never.

I got out of bed, pulled on my slippers, walked into the kitchen where the puppy played quietly by himself, and I whispered into his ear, "I'm going to take care of you no matter what."

And real love has happened for me ever since because real love is not a feeling. It's an act. And the act of loving is always worth it, regardless of the amount of time we're given and regardless of whether or not we ever get anything in return.

The End

What people are saying about *Somebunny To Love...*

"*Somebunny To Love* is absolutely wonderful! Somehow Lisa Soland was able to capture the true meaning of love in both a practical and Biblical way that is so simple yet so profound. Your children will not only enjoy the heartfelt story of love between a child and her pet, but they will also understand what the true meaning of love really is. I highly recommend this book for both young and old!"

– Mark Kirk, Pastor of Calvary Chapel Knoxville, Tennessee

"As is so beautifully affirmed in this story of bunnies and the humans with which they live, we tend to love that which we take care of – even if little is returned. I highly recommend this book for children who will either be taught for the first time or reinforced over time that love is a choice and, when given freely, is the only true love that exists."

– Brian Matthews, Licensed Marriage & Family Therapist, Texas

"Being an avid reader, I am overjoyed at each opportunity I receive to experience a new story. The special ones stay with me long after I finish reading them. *Somebunny to Love* is one of those special reads. The story touches on universal experiences of loss, sadness, and the accompanying questions of Why? Will this pain end? and Where is God? *Somebunny to Love* is one of the best treatments of grief I have read. I highly recommend it as a children's book, but I believe its uplifting message will speak to many adults, as well. It is pastoral without being preachy – a true work of love, grace and beauty."

– Rev. Sharon Roddy Waters, Disciples of Christ minister, Virginia

"Somebunny to Love, the beautiful tale of a young girl and her two pet rabbits, touches upon the complexities of human emotion in a heartfelt, straightforward manner. Masterfully written, it can be appreciated by one at any stage of life, for it speaks to our ever-growing awareness of what it means to give and receive love – and how love itself endures eternally."

– *Jeff Gordon, author and film historian, Texas*

"In Somebunny to Love, Lisa Soland creates an endearing coming of age story in which a young girl suffers the death of two rabbits and undergoes an inner struggle – in a world where pets have shorter life spans, is love worth the loss? With the help of wise parents and a strong better self, she comes to realize that the soulful risk we take for love is its own reward."

– *Bill Brown, poet, Tennessee*

ABOUT CLIMBING ANGEL PUBLISHING

Climbing Angel Publishing exists for the purpose of sharing stories of hope and encouragement.

Philippians 4:8
Jeremiah 29:11

The following works are available from Climbing Angel Publishing at www.ClimbingAngel.com, Amazon.com, and major bookstores.

The Christmas Tree Angel
The Unmade Moose
Thump
Somebunny To Love

CPSIA information can be obtained
at www.ICGtesting.com
Printed in the USA
LVOW05s1500120716

495926LV00033B/235/P